J

92965

DREAMWORKS
BEE MOVIE™

WHAT'S THE BUZZ?

HarperCollins®, ✦®, and HarperEntertainment™
are trademarks of HarperCollins Publishers.

Bee Movie: What's the Buzz?
Bee Movie™ & © 2007 DreamWorks Animation L.L.C.
Printed in the United States of America. All rights reserved.
No part of this book may be used or reproduced in any manner whatsoever without written
permission except in the case of brief quotations embodied in critical articles and reviews.
For information address HarperCollins Children's Books,
a division of HarperCollins Publishers,
1350 Avenue of the Americas, New York, NY 10019.
www.harpercollinschildrens.com

Library of Congress catalog card number: 2007930295
ISBN 978-0-06-125177-1

Cover design by Rick Farley
Interior design by John Sazaklis
❖
First Edition

DreamWorks

BEE MOVIE

BEE BULLETIN

THE MORNING EDITION

WHAT'S THE BUZZ?

Adapted by Judy Katschke

HarperEntertainment
An Imprint of HarperCollinsPublishers

BEE BULLETIN

CLASS OF 9:15
SPREADS ITS WINGS

CHAPTER ONE

Barry B. Benson wasn't usually a bee in a hurry, but today he had a need for speed. He was late for a graduation ceremony—his own!

Fluttering all four wings, Barry weaved his way through New Hive City until he reached his destination—the graduation hall. He raced up the aisle and slipped in line behind his best friend, Adam Flayman. Adam was tall and thin, and always wore the same wire-rimmed glasses.

"Well!" Adam said, his brown eyes peering over his glasses. "If it isn't Barry B. Benson—college graduate!"

"Can you believe that after today we're going to be the ones that make the honey in this hive?" Barry asked.

An excited *hum* filled the hall as Dean Buzzwell took his place behind a podium.

The dean glanced at the flipping numbers on the podium that displayed the time. There was a new graduating class every few minutes. "Welcome New Hive City graduating class of . . . nine-fifteen!"

Barry and Adam puffed out their striped chests proudly.

"So that concludes our graduation ceremonies," Dean Buzzwell said shortly, "and begins your career at Honex Industries."

Graduation hats were instantly replaced with hard hats. Rows of chairs suddenly morphed into a tour tram.

"You think we'll get to do anything today?" Barry asked as the tram moved forward.

"No," Adam said. "Day one's just orientation."

"Welcome to Honex," Trudy, the tour guide, said cheerily. "You, as a bee, have worked your whole life to get to the point where you can work for your whole life!"

The graduates listened as Trudy explained the honey-making process. Honey begins as nectar. The valiant pollen jocks go out into the world, retrieve it from flowers, and carry it to the hive where it is heated, cooled, and reheated before going through the filtering system.

"Finally it's color corrected, scent adjusted, and bubble contoured into this," Trudy went on, holding up a honey-filled test tube. "Soothing, sweet syrup with its distinctive golden glow. What you all know as—"

"H-o-n-e-y!" the graduates chanted.

"Our annual production is roughly two cups," Trudy explained. "We would have done three last year if it wasn't for those kids with a wiffle-ball bat. But we gave them a stinging they'll never forget!"

Next the tram took the graduates past all sorts of honey-making devices, such as the famous Krelman— a machine that scooped up honey drips.

To Adam, the Krelman was incredible. "Can anyone work there?" he asked.

"Yes," Trudy said. "The good news is, you'll stay in the job you pick for the rest of your life."

Barry's big blue eyes nearly popped out of his head. Suddenly, his whole life seemed so . . . boring.

The tram rambled on. The graduates laughed as it plunged down a steep drop. But Barry wasn't laughing. He knew bees were supposed to be busy, but was this all there was after college?

"So we graduate and five minutes later I have to decide what I'm going to do for the rest of my life?" Barry asked Adam when the tour ended.

"Everything's decided already," Adam said.

"Well, can I stop and think about it for just a second?" Barry asked.

"Sure, go ahead." Adam smirked. He waited a few seconds, then said, "Time's up. You're a bee making honey."

Barry gulped at the thought. He would do the same job tomorrow, and the next day, and the next day . . . until he was too old to do it anymore. That wasn't a future. That was a fate worse than a swatting.

CHAPTER TWO

Barry and Adam left Honex and crossed a busy street. Trucks, cars, and buses zoomed along. Pedestrian bees walked quickly this way and that. All around, life in New Hive City was running smoothly—just like it did every single day.

"Do you ever think things work a little *too* well around here?" Barry asked. His thoughts were suddenly interrupted by a booming voice.

"PLEASE CLEAR THE GATE! ROYAL NECTAR FORCE ON APPROACH!" a nearby bee announced.

"Hey!" Barry exclaimed. "Those are the pollen jocks!"

9

An army of burly bees zoomed through J-Gate, the main entrance to the hive. They were suited up in fighter pilot helmets with clear visors. They each wore a black jacket with a yellow stripe across the front. On the chest it had a set of wings—the symbol of the jocks. Their muscular legs were dusted with golden pollen.

"I've never seen them this close!" Adam said.

The nectar was removed from the jocks' backpacks. While it was loaded into trucks bound for Honex, their commander, Lou Duva, cheered them on. . . .

"You did great!" Lou exclaimed. "You're monsters! Sky freaks!"

Barry was impressed. Unlike most bees, pollen jocks could leave the hive to collect nectar from flowers. And though some swatted or sprayed souls never made it back, the brave bees were worshipped like rock stars.

"Outside the hive," Barry said longingly. "Flying who-knows-where, doing who-knows-what."

"Be a pollen jock, then," Adam suggested.

"Yeah, sure!" Barry scoffed. "All I've got to do is grow twice my height and put on seventy grams of rock-hard muscle."

As some jocks passed by, flecks of pollen drifted onto Barry and Adam. When two girl bees noticed the sparkling specks, they fluttered right over.

"You seem kind of small for pollen jocks," one girl said, giggling.

Barry and Adam traded excited looks. It wasn't often that girls paid attention to them.

"Yeah, we do a lot of freelance jocking," Barry said, playing along. "Rain-gutter hive, attic hive. . ."

A bunch of pollen jocks—named Buzz, Jackson, and Splitz—snickered as they eavesdropped on Barry and Adam's conversation.

"Look at those two!" Jackson whispered as he brushed a piece of pollen off his tall yellow boot.

"Couple of Hive Harrys," Splitz chuckled.

"Let's have some fun with them," Jackson said. Barry and Adam were still chatting up the girls as the jocks strolled over.

"Little gusty out there, wasn't it, comrades?" Buzz boomed.

Barry froze when he saw the jocks. He wanted to run, but his legs felt like jelly. So he decided instead to play along. . . .

"Yeah . . . gusty." Barry gulped.

"We're going to hit a sunflower patch about six miles from here tomorrow," Buzz continued. "Maybe you're not up for it."

"Maybe I am!" Barry said.

"You are not!" Adam hissed, trying to save his friend from certain death.

"We're going, oh nine hundred at J-Gate," Buzz said.

"What do you think, Adam?" Barry asked.

"I would love to," Adam said, pulling nervously at his sweater. "But I had planned on not being dead tomorrow!"

Barry watched as the jocks walked away laughing. Did he just agree to go flying with them?

What was he thinking?

That evening as Barry ate dinner, he didn't have to think about his future. His family was doing that for him.

"Have you decided what you're interested in?" his father, Martin, asked as he adjusted his glasses. "Heating and cooling? Pouring?"

"You know, Dad," Barry said. "The more I think about it . . . maybe the honey field just isn't right for me."

Martin stared at his son. Did he have beeswax in his ears? Did Barry just say what he thought he said?

"There's only honey, son!" Martin said loudly.

But before Barry could reply, Janet, Barry's mom, entered carrying a tray of honey-sweetened drinks.

"To honey!" Janet said as she raised a glass.

"To honey," Barry sighed, slowly lifting his drink.

He'd better get used to this. Tomorrow would be the beginning of a lifelong career—and the end of his freedom.

"I can't believe we're starting work today," Adam said the next morning.

The two friends were entering Honex. But to Barry, they might as well have been entering a can of Raid.

"Step right up and make your choice!" Dean Buzzwell boomed from the job placement counter.

Barry studied the chart listing the different available jobs: heating, cooling, stunts, stirring. Next to each job were the words *open*, *pending*, or *closed*.

"Any chance of getting on the Krelman?" Adam asked.

Buzzwell turned to the chart just as the Krelman job flipped from OPEN to CLOSED.

"Sorry," Buzzwell said. "The Krelman just closed out."

Adam looked down, disappointed.

Suddenly the Krelman job flipped from CLOSED . . . to OPEN!

"What happened?" Adam asked.

"Whenever a bee dics, that's an opening," Buzzwell explaincd.

Whenever a bee dies? That's all Barry  needed to hear. While Adam made a decision, Barry made his. He wasn't going to be just an average bee. For once in his life, he was going for the gold.

Sweet gold nectar!

CHAPTER THREE

Barry stood by J-Gate watching the jocks go through their preflight checks. They pulled on their helmets and jackets. He had to do this. Or else he'd always be just a pollen jock wannabee.

Barry's thoughts were interrupted as his antennae rang. It was Adam calling—and he was frantic!

"Where are you?" Adam's voice cried.

"I'm going out," Barry whispered into his antennae.

"Out where?" Adam whispered.

"Out there," Barry answered. "It's a one-time thing. I'm going to try."

"You're going to die!" Adam screamed.

Barry refused to be discouraged. He said good-bye to Adam, took a deep breath, then strolled over to the pollen jocks.

"Hi, guys!" Barry said.

The pollen jocks snickered.

"Hold it, son!" Lou Duva said. "Flight deck's restricted."

"It's okay, Lou," Jackson said. "We're taking him up."

"Okay!" Lou called out. "Watch out for brooms, hockey sticks, dogs, birds, bears, and bats."

Bears? Bats? Barry gulped. The outside world was scarier than he thought.

Lou gave Barry a stern look. "And there is absolutely, positively no talking to humans!"

"Ready for this, hotshot?" Splitz asked Barry.

Barry was ready—to fly home. But he couldn't let the guys see him sweat.

"Bring it on," Barry squeaked.

"Launch positions!" Lou announced.

The jocks assessed their gear: Wind. Check! Antennae. Check! Nectar pack. Check! Wings, stinger—check, check!

"Let's move it out, ladies!" Lou shouted.

With a hearty *hum* the pollen jocks flipped down their goggles and began fluttering their wings. A flight-deck bee gave the hand signals as the jocks took off through the J-Gate. Barry followed, not knowing what to expect.

But as they zoomed outside, Barry's heart felt light.

"I'm out!" Barry yelled excitedly.

For once he felt fast and free. Barry's world exploded in color. There were vibrant plants and flowers everywhere he looked. Below him was an amazing sight—humans! Riding bikes, jogging, pushing baby carriages, and walking dogs.

"We have roses visual," Splitz reported in the sky. "Bring it around thirty degrees and hold."

"Roses!" Barry exclaimed.

Suddenly Barry remembered—that's what he was there for. Pollen.

"Thirty degrees, roger," Jackson said. "Bringing it around."

Barry watched in awe as one jock used a powerful stem-sucking gun to draw nectar from a flower.

"What a machine that is!" Barry cried.

Barry trailed the jocks as they skimmed the surface of a pond and soared high above a bubbling fountain. As they flew over a green field in fancy formation, Buzz detected a cluster of yellow daisies.

"These flowers seem to be on the move!" Buzz reported.

The jocks and Barry touched down to inspect the strange daisies. They had no clue the field was really a tennis court. Or that the moving yellow flowers were really tennis balls.

"Smells good!" Splitz said, sniffing a tennis ball. "Not like a flower, but I like it."

"I'm loving this color!" Jackson exclaimed.

Barry landed on one of the tennis balls and collapsed from exhaustion. All this flying was hard work, and the ball felt so soft and fuzzy.

"Get off of there!" Jackson shouted.

Barry tried to lift himself off. But his body stuck to the fuzzy ball!

"I have a problem. . . ." Barry gulped.

But Barry's problems were just beginning. Out of nowhere, a giant human hand swooped down and grabbed the ball. Barry groaned as he was lifted high into the air. That stirrer job at Honex seemed more appealing by the second!

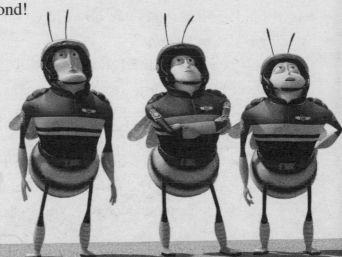

CHAPTER FOUR

"This could be bad," Buzz murmured to the pollen jocks as they watched Barry.

A human named Vanessa was in the middle of a heated tennis match with her friend Ken. She didn't notice the tiny bee stuck to her ball. She tucked a stray hair behind her ear and began bouncing it on the court.

Thunk! Thunk! Thunk!

Barry's bee brain rattled each time the ball hit the court. Sheer luck kept him from being totally squished.

It was Vanessa's serve. She tossed the ball into the air and whammed it with her racket.

"Whoaaa!" Barry cried as he flew toward Ken.

The volley was on. The pollen jocks watched as an exhausted Barry tried unsuccessfully to steer the ball away from the rackets.

"Help meeeee!" Barry called.

It was up to the pollen jocks to save the day. Just as Ken was about to swing, Jackson uttered a loud, "Ahem!"

As Ken turned to see where the sound had come from, he missed the oncoming ball. Barry was still hanging on.

Barry screamed as the ball whistled away from the court. It bounced off a hot-dog stand and into the middle of the street. One bounce sent the ball flying against the grille of a car!

The ball flew through the grille as a screaming Barry was sucked inside. After a wild ride past pistons and

whirling vanes, Barry popped into the passenger section, packed with a vacationing family.

"There's a bee in the car!" the mom shouted.

Barry dodged swatting kids and a snapping, slobbering dog. He thought things couldn't get worse, until . . .

"Little varmint!" Grandma growled. "I'll nonstick Cook 'N Spray him!"

Barry gulped. Granny had a can of Cook 'N Spray, and wasn't afraid to use it!

"Kill it!" Mom yelled.

A blast of cooking spray coated everything . . . except Barry. He darted around the car, bounced off the dog and out the sunroof.

"I've got to get home!" Barry groaned. He flew up and into the air. But soon he felt a few drops. Rain.

As the rain got heavier, Barry's wings went limp.

"Mayday!" Barry shouted. "Bee going down!"

He landed with a thud on a colorful window box and crawled through an open window just as four humans were entering the apartment. It was Vanessa and Ken from the tennis court! They were with their friends Andy and Anna.

"Ken, can you close the window, please?" Vanessa asked. She had short brown hair and green eyes and looked a lot nicer than Barry remembered.

Barry ducked behind the drapes just as Ken shut the window. The last thing he needed was another run-in with humans. He tried zooming out the window but smashed again and again against an invisible wall—glass. Barry had never seen such a thing before.

There had to be a way out. He glanced up and saw something glowing above him.

"The sun!" Barry said. "Maybe that's a way out."

Barry zoomed up. He knocked into a lightbulb and zigzagged downward, landing in a bowl of guacamole. Andy dipped his chip, scooping up a dollop of avocado, and—

"Beeeee!" Ken shouted.

"Kill it!" Anna yelled.

Barry froze. Ken sprang into action. He took off his boots and put one on each hand.

"Stand back!" Ken growled, his brown eyes narrowing.

Barry's bee blood ran cold. He had survived tennis rackets, a slobbering dog, and a spray-can-packing granny. Could he survive a pair of size-ten-and-a-half boots?

BEE BULLETIN
THE MORNING EDITION

BEE BREAKS LAW, TALKS TO HUMAN

CHAPTER FIVE

Barry squeezed his eyes shut. But just as he prepared for the ultimate squish . . .

"Don't kill him!"

Barry's eyes opened to see Vanessa, her hand stopping Ken.

"Why does his life have any less value than yours?" Vanessa argued. She grabbed a glass and flipped it over Barry. Then she slipped a catalog under the glass.

"There you go, little guy," Vanessa said as she opened the window and slid Barry onto the window box.

It was still pouring as Barry sat among the flowers, trying to stay dry. Through the open window, he could see Vanessa saying good night to her friends.

As Barry watched Vanessa, Lou's words echoed in his head. *There is absolutely, positively NO talking to humans!* Barry knew it was a bee law, but he had to thank Vanessa for saving his life.

Zipping into the apartment, he hid behind a row of jars in the kitchen. As Vanessa walked by, Barry popped out and said, "Hi."

Vanessa dropped the stack of dishes she was holding. "You're talking!" She gasped, jumping backward. She looked curiously at Barry. "It's just . . . you're a bee!"

"I just want you to know that I'm grateful," Barry said matter-of-factly. "And I'm going to leave now."

"Wait!" Vanessa said. "How did you learn to talk?"

"The same way you did, I guess," Barry said. "Mama, Dada, honey . . ."

Vanessa laughed. "That's funny!"

"Bees are funny!" Barry said. "If we didn't laugh, we'd cry—with what we have to deal with."

Vanessa talked Barry into staying. After all, he was no ordinary insect. Soon they were sitting together in her rooftop garden, sharing a huge piece of cake.

"I want to do my part for the hive," Barry said. "But I can't do it the way my parents want."

"I know how you feel," Vanessa said. "My parents wanted me to be a doctor or a lawyer. But I wanted to be a florist."

A florist? Barry knew there was something about Vanessa he liked.

"This has been great," Barry said as he got ready to leave. It was more than great though. Today was the best day of Barry's life, and he had Vanessa to thank for that.

"I guess I'll see you around," Barry said slowly as he took off.

The rain had stopped. As Barry flew home to his Central Park hive he wanted to shout for joy. He had left New Hive City and found amazing things—kites, cars, fields of flowers. But the most amazing thing about the outside world was a human . . . Vanessa.

CHAPTER SIX

The next morning, Barry was sitting inside Adam's Honex office.

"I can't believe you were with humans!" Adam said, shocked. "What were they like? Did they try to kill you like on TV?"

"Some of them," Barry said.

"OK, you did it, and now you're back," Adam said, suddenly serious. "You can pick out your job, and everything can be normal."

Barry knew things couldn't be normal from now on. "I met someone," he said. "She's a human."

Adam's stripes practically zigzagged with shock.

"Oh, no!" Adam cried. "You wouldn't break a bee law!" Adam slammed a tiny black fist on his desk.

"Her name is Vanessa," Barry went on. "And she's a florist!"

"This is over," Adam said. Florist or not, bees and humans could not be friends. But then Barry pulled out a cake crumb.

"Eat this," he said, shoving the crumb in Adam's mouth. Adam chewed the crumb, his eyes wide with excitement.

"This is not over. What was that?" Adam asked.

"They call it a crumb," Barry said, smiling. "And that's not even what they eat. That just falls off what they eat." Adam could not listen to another word.

"You're talking to *humans*. Humans that attack *our* homes with power washers and M-80s!" Adam exclaimed. "You have to start thinking *bee*, my friend. Thinking bee."

It was useless, though. All Barry could think about was the outside world.

It wasn't long before Barry ventured out of the hive again. Passersby took swats at him as he strolled down the street with Vanessa.

"You must want to sting all those jerks," Vanessa said.

Barry shook his head as they entered a busy supermarket. Humans didn't realize that stinging was serious business for bees—a matter of life and death.

"We try not to sting," Barry explained. "It's usually fatal for us."

Barry hopped on some cardboard boxes in the middle of the aisle. He was about to walk over a strip of masking tape when—

WAP!

Barry groaned as he stumbled across the box. Through spinning eyeballs he could see Hector, a stock boy with a backward hat, holding a rolled-up newspaper.

"Barry, are you okay?" Vanessa cried.

"Whew!" Barry gasped.

Vanessa grabbed Hector's newspaper and whacked him hard on the head. "What is wrong with you?" she demanded.

"It's a bug!" Hector cried, rubbing his head.

"He's not bothering anybody," Vanessa said. "Get out of here, you creep!"

Hector walked off, mumbling. Barry studied the newspaper in Vanessa's hand. He was lucky it was only a ten-page circular, not a bulky fashion magazine.

He had lost a cousin that way.

But just as Barry was feeling better, he spotted

something that made his jaw drop—a wall of shelves filled with . . . honey jars.

"What in the name of Mighty Hercules is this?" Barry cried in horror. "Why is this here?"

"For people." Vanessa shrugged. "We eat it."

"How do you even get it?" Barry asked.

"Well . . . bees make it," Vanessa answered.

"And it's hard to make!" Barry cried. "There's heating, and cooling, and stirring, and filtering—"

"It's just honey, Barry," Vanessa said.

Just honey?

"This is stealing!" Barry yelled.

As Barry ripped the label off a jar of honey he realized what his new job would be. It wouldn't be stirring or filtering or operating that Krelman thing.

"I'm going to get to the bottom of this!" he declared.

BEE BULLETIN

THE EVENING EDITION

SHOW ME THE HONEY!

CHAPTER SEVEN

Barry was on a secret mission. So as not to be seen, he blacked out the yellow lines on his sweater with a magic marker. He could see Hector in the storeroom cutting open boxes with a knife—boxes filled with honey jars.

"Just honey, huh?" Barry muttered. He zoomed over to Hector and stared him straight in the eye.

"Who's your supplier?" Barry demanded.

Hector backed up against a wall, his arms held up to his face in shock. "We were just about to bring all this honey back!" he cried. "To you bees!"

Then, out of nowhere, Hector grabbed a pushpin and pointed it at Barry. With a weapon in hand, Hector changed his tone. "You're too late," he sneered. "It's ours now!"

Barry whipped around and used his trusty stinger to fence. What followed was a heart-pounding duel. Barry and Hector crossed swords.

"Where's the honey coming from?" Barry asked. He knocked the pushpin from Hector's hand and pressed his stinger against Hector's nose. "Tell me!"

Hector pointed to a truck. "It comes from Honey Farms," he stammered fearfully.

That was all Barry needed to hear. He chased the truck out of the parking lot and onto a busy street. To gain speed, he grabbed onto a bicycle messenger's backpack. Using the bungee cord as a slingshot, he launched himself toward the racing truck.

Barry landed on the windshield, where he found himself surrounded by squashed, dead bugs!

"Oh, the horror of it all!" Barry cried.

But a few bugs were still alive—like a big red ladybug bound for Tacoma and a mosquito named Mooseblood with a long red nose

Barry watched as the world in front of him whizzed by. It had been a long, tiring day. He climbed into the truck's horn and was soon fast asleep.

Until . . . *BEEEEEP!*

Barry's eyes snapped open as the truck shot past a sign reading, HONEY FARMS—SCHOOL GROUP TOURS AVAILABLE!

This was the place!

Barry zipped out of the horn. He heard the voice of Freddy, a tour guide, in the distance. . . .

"This is an apiary, kids," Freddy said, holding a wooden box. "It's a beehive made out of the cheapest wood we can find!"

Barry watched as Freddy tossed the empty "hive" onto the ground, smashing it to bits.

"Why do you keep bees?" a boy named Timmy asked.

"Because they make the honey," Freddy replied. "And then we make the money."

"Just as I thought," Barry muttered.

"Don't they sting you?" a boy named Bobby asked.

"They try," Freddy said. "But all we've got to do is give them one of these."

Freddy held up a bulky metal contraption. "It's a smoker!" he said. "Knocks them right out!"

Barry's stinger shook furiously. If only he could knock Freddy out!

"By the time the bees wake up, the honey is ours," Freddy explained. "And they're back to the flowers."

It seemed too horrible to be true. Barry had to get closer to see for himself. He flew onto the brim of Freddy's hat. From there he watched as the tour guide pointed the smoker at apiary boxes filled with bees. Then—

WHOOOOOOOOSH!

Sick to his stomach, Barry watched as Freddy blasted each wooden box with smoke. This was worse than anything bears had done to bees. Ever.

But just when Barry thought the atrocities couldn't get worse, he spotted hundreds of apiary boxes stretching as far as the eye could see.

"Oh, no!" Barry cried. "Bee honey—our honey—being brazenly stolen on a massive scale!"

First he would deliver the proof. Then he would deliver justice—for all bees everywhere.

CHAPTER EIGHT

Barry knew it wouldn't be easy. But he was determined to sue the entire honey industry and save his fellow bees from their apiaries. In no time Barry's crusade made newspaper headlines and Hive at Five, the evening news. . . .

"Good evening, I'm Bob Bumble," the anchor bee announced, his silver hair slicked back. "In our top story, a tricounty bee, Barry Benson, is alleging that humans have been stealing our honey, packaging it, and profiting from it illegally."

Barry became one busy bee. When he wasn't giving interviews, he and Adam were busy reading legal books in Vanessa's flower shop.

"Do you realize how big this is going to be?"

Vanessa asked. "Are you sure you want to go through with it?"

"Am I sure?" Barry huffed as he walked across the pages of one of the books. "When I'm done with humans they won't even be able to say, 'Honey, I'm home,' without paying a fee!"

Finally the trial of the century was in session. Barry, Adam, and Vanessa sat side by side in the courtroom. A chill ran through Barry as the defense lawyer, Layton T. Montgomery, entered the courtroom. . . .

"Well!" Montgomery said, shaking a packet of honey. "If it isn't the B-team!"

"All rise!" the bailiff said. "The Honorable Judge Bumbleton presiding."

Everyone stood as the judge entered the courtroom. She sat down and cleared her throat.

"*Barry B. Benson vs. the Honey Industry* is now in session," Judge Bumbleton said. "Mr. Benson, you're representing all the bees of the world?"

"Yes, Your Honor," Barry replied.

"And Mr. Montgomery," Judge Bumbleton said. "You're representing all five major food companies?"

"An honor!" Mr. Montgomery declared.

After the opening statements, it was time to call the first witnesses. Barry called Mr. Klauss Vanderhayden of Honey Farms to the stand. . . .

"So, Mr. Vanderhayden," Barry said, looking down at his notes. "I see you also own Honey Burton and Hon-Ron."

"Yes," Vanderhayden said. "They provide beekeepers for our farm."

"Beekeepers!" Barry exclaimed. "I don't imagine you employ any bee-freers, do you?"

"No," Vanderhayden said.

"Not only that," Barry went on. "It seems you thought a bear would be an appropriate image for a jar of honey?"

"They're very lovable creatures," Vanderhayden said.

"Oh, really?" Barry said smugly.

The door swung open. Vanessa and her janitor were pulling a real-live bear into the courtroom. The snarling bear wore a collar with a chain attached to both sides!

"Bears kill bees!" Barry shouted as the bear lunged at Vanderhayden. "How would you like his big hairy head crashing into your living room?"

More witnesses testified: Hector the stock boy. A rock star named Sting. But the biggest moment in the trial came when Barry himself was called to the stand. . . .

"Mr. Benson," Montgomery began. "I've seen a bee movie or two. Doesn't the queen give birth to all the bee children in the hive?"

Barry had no idea where Montgomery was going with his questioning. "Yeah," he said. "But—"

Montgomery pointed to Mr. and Mrs. Benson, who were sitting in the courtroom. "So those aren't even your real parents!" he declared.

"Yes, they are!" Barry cried.

A heated hum filled the bee gallery. But no one was as swarming mad as Adam!

"He's insulting bees!" Adam shouted. "I'm going to pincushion the guy!"

Montgomery turned around and bent over. Barry could see him glancing over his shoulder and winking at his team.

"Adam—don't!" Barry cried. "It's what he wants!"

Too late.

Adam zoomed across the courtroom, straight toward Montgomery. The jury gasped as Adam's stinger speared the defense attorney right in his butt.

"I'm hit! I'm hit!" Montgomery cried.

Barry stared at Adam hanging by his stinger. What was his hotheaded friend thinking? Didn't he know that stinging often meant death for the bee?

"See?" Montgomery shouted. "Bees are striped savages! Stinging is all they know!"

The jury reacted in horror.

Montgomery's sneaky strategy had turned the trial against the bees. But all Barry could think about was Adam. He rushed to his friend's side.

"I can't feel my legs!" Adam gasped, his antennae going limp.

"Adam, stay with me!" Barry pleaded.

He could deal with losing the case. But there was no way he could deal with losing his best friend.

BEE BULLETIN
THE MORNING EDITION

BEE SURVIVES STING

CHAPTER NINE

ater that day, Barry entered Adam's hospital room with a get-well bouquet. Adam sat up in his bed. The doctors had managed to remove his stinger, which saved his life.

"Hey, buddy," Barry said.

"Hey," Adam said weakly. "I blew the whole case, didn't I?" He could barely open his eyes.

"It doesn't matter," Barry said. "The most important thing is that you're alive."

"I would have been better off dead!" Adam cried. "Look at me!"

Adam tossed aside his sheets. In the place where his stinger had been there was a blue plastic toothpick from the hospital cafeteria. It looked like a sword.

Barry winced. *That's got to hurt!*

Just then, a swirl of smoke drifted in from an open window. Barry glanced outside and saw three humans smoking on the sidewalk.

"Could you get a nurse to close that window?" Adam coughed. "Bees don't smoke!"

Smoke? The word made Barry's antennae perk up.

"Adam!" he cried. "That's our case!"

As soon as Adam was discharged, court was back in session. But Barry and Vanessa were nowhere to be found.

"Where is the rest of your team, Mr. Flayman?" Judge Bumbleton asked.

Adam fumbled with his plastic stinger.

"Well, Your Honor," Adam said, trying to stall the judge. "I actually heard a funny story. . . ."

Montgomery rolled to the judge's desk in an unusual wheelchair. He wore a neck brace and looked disgusted.

"Your Honor!" Montgomery objected. "Haven't these ridiculous bugs taken up enough of this court's valuable time?"

"But we have a terrific case!" Adam said.

"Where is your proof?" Montgomery demanded. "Show me the smoking gun!"

Did he say smoking gun?

The doors opened and Barry flew into the courtroom. Behind him was Vanessa, a beekeeper's smoker in her hands.

"Here is your smoking gun!" Barry shouted.

"What is that?" Judge Bumbleton asked.

"It's a bee smoker!" Barry explained.

Montgomery grabbed the smoker. "This couldn't hurt a fly, let alone a bee," he scoffed.

To prove his point, Montgomery aimed the smoke toward the bee gallery. One by one the bees coughed and dropped to the ground.

"Is this what nature intended for us?" Barry demanded. "To be addicted to smoke machines in man-made wooden work camps?"

Barry flew to the jury rail and began to shout, "Ladies and gentleman, please, free these bees!"

"Free the bees! Free the bees!" the jury chanted.

Chaos erupted in the courtroom. Judge Bumbleton pounded her gavel and shouted, "The court finds in favor of the bees!"

"We won!" Barry cried.

Vanessa high-fived Barry, sending him crashing into the table. But nothing could keep Barry down. He had won the case—and a sweet victory for the bees!

"This will upset the balance of nature!" Montgomery warned. "You'll regret this, Benson!"

Barry flew outside and met a swarm of reporters. Adam turned to Vanessa, a look of worry on his long face.

"We've been living the bee way a long time," Adam said. "Twenty-seven million years."

What if Montgomery was right?

CHAPTER TEN

After the trial, Barry went from zero to hero. Reporters couldn't get enough of the bee who had brought the honey industry to its knees.

"Congratulations on your victory," a reporter said. "What are you going to demand as a settlement?"

"This was never about money," Barry explained. "We're going to demand a complete shutdown of all honey-producing bee work camps."

The reporters held their mikes and scribbled in their pads as Barry went on.

"Honey does not belong in lozenges or glazed over hams."

Soon the honey raids began. Armies of tough bees and human agents raided Honey Farms, locking it up for good. All bee smokers were collected and locked up, too. Imprisoned bees were finally free to leave their apiaries.

But the crackdowns didn't end with the farms. Supermarkets were cleared of all honey products. Bears in the woods were roughed up as agents looked for secret honey stashes. Little gray-haired ladies at tea parties weren't even safe.

Barry watched his dream come true. Honey was gushing into the hive every second and it wasn't for humans anymore. It was for bees . . . and that was good.

But as more and more honey oozed in, it rose dangerously past the three-cup mark—and that was bad.

"Cease all honey production until further notice!" Buzzwell ordered.

The Honex whistle blew. It was the end of the workday—maybe the end of all workdays.

Adam was clearing out his office when Barry zoomed in.

"You wouldn't believe how much honey is out there!" Barry cheered. "And now it's ours again!"

"Really?" Adam said. "That's great."

But from the look on his face, it was clear that Adam thought it was anything but.

"We had a unique purpose, Barry," Adam sighed. "So what if we weren't the only ones who liked honey? We were still the only ones who could make it."

"But now we don't *need* to make it!" Barry said.

"No," Adam said as they left the factory. "Now we don't need to do anything."

Barry glanced back at Honex. The factory that once buzzed with energy was now deserted. And bees weren't the only ones out of work. Without bees there were no flowers. And without flowers, no flower shops.

Later that day, Vanessa led Barry up the stairs to her rooftop.

"What did you want to show me, Vanessa?" Barry asked.

When they reached the top she flung the door wide open and said, "This!"

Barry gasped. All of the flowers in Vanessa's garden were shriveled and lifeless. But, even worse, all of Central Park was now brown. The once colorful plants and trees were dying.

"They're wilting," Barry said sadly.

"Whose fault do you think that is?" Vanessa asked.

"Mine," Barry admitted. "But I didn't think that bees not needing to make honey would affect all these other things."

"It's not just flowers," Vanessa said. "It's fruits, vegetables. They all need bees."

Barry felt awful. His actions had affected fruits, vegetables, and flowers. But he also felt awful about Honex and New Hive City. He had wanted the lives of bees to be better. He didn't want bees to have to work *so* hard. But now everyone was just lounging around the hive, doing nothing.

"I know this is partly my fault." Vanessa sighed as she turned toward the door. "I'm sorry Barry, but I've got to get going."

Barry lowered his eyes as Vanessa left the rooftop. Why did he always have to question everything? Why couldn't he just become a stirrer like his dad?

CHAPTER ELEVEN

Barry knew he had to fix the mess he made. He shot down the staircase and out of the building, just as Vanessa was stepping into a cab.

"Where are you going, Vanessa?" Barry asked.

"To the final Tournament of Roses Parade in Pasadena," Vanessa replied. "They moved it up to this weekend because all the flowers are dying."

"I'm sorry," Barry said. "I never meant for it to turn out like this!"

"I know," Vanessa sighed. "Me neither."

The cab pulled away, leaving Barry alone on the sidewalk. If only someone would swat him and take him out of his misery.

As Barry turned, his eye caught Vanessa's shut-down flower shop. Hanging in the window was a poster for the Rose Bowl Parade.

Roses!

"Roses are flowers!" Barry shouted as he flew after the cab. "Flowers, bees, pollen!"

Vanessa rolled down the window and Barry zipped inside. "That's why this is the last parade," she said.

"Maybe not!" Barry said. "If they have roses, the roses have pollen. If we could get that pollen and bring it back, that's all we need!"

"You mean repollinate Central Park?" Vanessa asked.

"It's a start!" Barry said hopefully.

Once in Pasadena the friends put plan B into action. Sporting Barry as a pin, Vanessa approached an armed guard in front of the staging area.

"Vanessa Bloome, official floral business," Vanessa said.

The guard stepped aside to let Vanessa through. "Nice pin, by the way," he said.

Barry and Vanessa moved through the bustling staging area. Standing in a row were fragrant floats decorated with colorful roses.

There were sports floats, history floats—even fairy-tale floats. Barry and Vanessa stopped in front of a Princess and the Pea float. On it was a pile of mattresses made of roses and a snooty-looking girl dressed as a princess.

"We may be able to pull that off," Vanessa whispered.

"All we need to do is deprincessify it," Barry whispered back.

In the blink of an eye, Barry was suited up in a round green costume, hovering over the float.

"What are you?" the princess cried as she stared at the fluttering green blob.

"I believe I'm the pea," Barry said.

"There is no pea!" the princess scoffed. "It's supposed to be under the mattresses."

"Not in this fairy tale, sweetheart," Barry said.

The princess turned to get the marshall. But just as she was about to step off the float, Vanessa yanked away the ladder. Barry watched as the princess took a royal spill.

With the princess down for the count, Vanessa jumped aboard. Quickly she pulled on the princess hat while Barry reviewed their plan. . . .

"OK, now we remove the float from the parade without arousing suspicion," Barry said.

A marching band led the floats down the parade route. But Barry and Vanessa had other ideas. They steered their float off course, crashing it through a fence.

"We have only twenty minutes to catch the next plane!" Vanessa said.

It was all systems go.

Barry and Vanessa had gotten their float onto the California freeway. Now they just had to get it back to New York.

BEE BULLETIN

THE EVENING EDITION

FLOWER POWER!

The Princess and the Pea float pulled up to the airport curb. While Vanessa distracted the redcap, Barry secretly switched tags from a passenger's bag to the float.

It was a crazy plan, but it worked. Soon Barry, Vanessa, and the last roses on earth were aboard a plane bound for New York City.

"Attention passengers," a voice said over the PA system. "This is Captain Scott. I'm afraid we have a bit of bad weather in New York. We're going to be experiencing a couple of hours' delay."

Bad news. Without water, the flowers wouldn't make it.

"I've got to talk to these guys," Barry said.

He fluttered to the cockpit door. Through it he could hear the flight attendant chatting with the pilots.

"Hey!" Barry yelled, pounding on the door.

As the flight attendant stepped out of the door, Barry flit past her into the cockpit.

"Excuse me, Captain," Barry said. "I am in a real situation here!"

Captain Scott was studying the altitude indicator. He glanced at the copilot and said, "What did you say, Hal?"

"I didn't say anything," Hal replied.

Captain Scott spotted Barry hovering behind him. "Bee!" he yelled.

"Don't freak out!" Barry pleaded.

Too late. Both pilots began scrambling for any bee-buster they could find.

Captain Scott grabbed a DustBuster vacuum cleaner. He aimed it around the cockpit, trying to suck up Barry. Instead he sucked Hal's toupee right off his head!

Barry hopped over Hal's bald head to avoid the swinging vacuum cleaner. Finally Captain Scott brought it down with a smash—on Hal's nose!

Hal fell out of his chair, hitting the life raft release button. The giant raft pumped up with air and flew into Captain Scott, knocking him out cold!

Barry groaned. He flew to the speaker system. Then, using his best pilot voice, he announced, "This is your captain speaking. Would a Vanessa Bloome report to the cockpit? And please hurry!"

Vanessa raced down the aisle into the cockpit. When she saw the damage, she screamed, "What happened in here?"

"I tried to talk to them!" Barry babbled. "But then there was a DustBuster, and a toupee, and a raft exploded. Now one's bald, one's in a boat—"

"Is this a bee joke?" Vanessa demanded.

The voice of Bud Ditchwater, air traffic controller, crackled over the intercom.

"This is JFK control tower," Bud's voice reported. "Flight three five six, what's your status?"

Barry gulped. Did he really want to know?

"This is Vanessa Bloome," Vanessa said. "I'm a florist."

"Where's the pilot?" Bud asked.

"He's unconscious," Vanessa explained. "So is the copilot."

"Not good," Bud said. "Is there anyone onboard who has flight experience?"

Barry's eyes darted around the cockpit. The plane was nothing more than a big metal bee with giant wings and huge engines.

"As a matter of fact . . . ," Barry declared. "There is!"

CHAPTER THIRTEEN

Who said that?" Bud asked.

"Barry Benson," Vanessa replied.

"From the honey trial?" Bud groaned.

Barry ignored Bud and turned to Vanessa.

"We're going to land this plane," he said. "I'll just do what I do, and you copy me with the wings of the plane."

Vanessa took her place at the controls. She grabbed the throttle levers. Then she waited for Barry's instructions.

"All right, pull back," Barry said, hovering in the air next to Vanessa. "See how my head's coming up here a little?"

Vanessa worked the throttles. But outside the windshield, dark clouds loomed ahead.

"We're heading straight into a storm!" Vanessa cried.

"There's no time to go around it," Barry said.

Thunder boomed. Lightning flashed. Vanessa gritted her teeth as she piloted the plane through the storm.

Back at Air Traffic Control, Hive at Five was already on the scene.

"We have two individuals at the controls of a jumbo jet with absolutely no flight experience," Bud told the reporter, Jeanette Chung.

"Just a minute, Mr. Ditchwater," Jeanette said. "There's a honeybee on the plane. Isn't that your only hope right now?"

"According to the law of aviation, a bee shouldn't be able to fly at all," Bud said. "Their wings are too small, their bodies are too big, and I'm not crazy about their stripes, either."

Bud's radio was still on and Barry could hear every word.

"Haven't we heard this a million times?" Barry shouted to Bud.

Upon hearing Barry's voice, Jeanette turned to her cameraman. "Get this on the air!" she said.

In minutes all the bees of New Hive City were glued to their TV sets, listening to Barry defend their species.

"Mr. Ditchwater," Barry explained, "our whole lives

are based on things we can't do. That's why I want to get bees back to doing what makes us bees. Working together!"

Barry's family and Adam watched the drama unfold. So did Dean Buzzwell and the pollen jocks.

"We're not made of Jell-O," Barry went on. "We get behind a fellow. Black and yellow."

New Hive City exploded in cheers.

"How are we doing on time?" Barry asked Vanessa.

Vanessa glanced at Barry fluttering beside her.

"Not great," Vanessa said. In a little while all the flowers would be wilted.

Barry knew the situation was grim. What he didn't know was that help was on the way.

"All of you!" Lou Duva shouted as he led the pollen jocks to J-Gate. "Let's move it out!"

CHAPTER FOURTEEN

There was little time and little fuel. Barry and Vanessa worked hard at saving the flowers and the plane.

"Left, right, down, hover!" Barry shouted at Vanessa's side.

"Hover?" Vanessa cried.

"Forget hover," Barry said.

A bolt of lightning zapped the plane. The radio fizzled as it shorted out. Flight 356 had lost contact!

Vanessa maneuvered the plane through wind and rain. She gripped the controls so tightly, her knuckles turned white. Blue skies appeared ahead, but they were not in the clear yet. . . .

"We have to land soon or we'll be out of fuel," Vanessa said.

"How much fuel is left?" Barry asked.

One engine turbine stopped. Then the other. The plane lurched.

"I'm going to guess none," Vanessa said. "What's going to happen to us?"

"I'm going to guess . . . we're done," Barry gulped.

Flight 356 began to drop. But just when Barry and Vanessa thought they were goners, the plane stopped in midair. Like magic, it flipped back into position and glided ahead.

"How is the plane flying?" Vanessa gasped.

"I don't know," Barry said.

A voice crackled over Barry's antennae. "Hey, Benson! Have you got any flowers for a happy occasion?"

Huh? Barry glanced out the windshield to see Lou, Buzz, Splitz, and Jackson flying alongside the cockpit. They led a gigantic swarm of bees who were holding the plane up.

"The pollen jocks!" Barry exclaimed.

Vanessa could hear Lou over her headset.

"All right, you two," Lou said. "What do you say we drop this tin can on the blacktop?"

"What blacktop?" Vanessa cried. "I can't see anything."

Neither could Barry. But it wasn't all hopeless.

Waiting on the runway was Adam—with another swarm of bees.

"Come on, Barry!" Adam yelled to the air. "You have to think bee. Thinking bee. Thinking bee!"

The swarm fell into formation. Slowly a huge black-and-yellow flower began emerging on the runway.

"Thinking bee! Thinking bee!" the bees chanted.

Up in the plane Barry was getting weird vibes. He couldn't explain it, but his bee instincts were taking over.

"Vanessa, bring the nose of the plane down," Barry blurted. "Guys—cut your power by fifty percent."

Lou Duva gave the command. As visibility improved, the tarmac came into view. A flower of bees slowly appeared through the mist.

"Put some lights on that!" Bud ordered.

Aircraft landing lights flashed along the sides of the runway. From the plane Barry made out the black-and-yellow flower, fully illuminated!

"Aim for the flower, Vanessa!" Barry said. "Ready, boys? Give me full reverse. Vanessa, flaps down!"

Vanessa and the bees followed Barry's instructions. The plane turned sharply. Below in the cargo hold, the Princess and the Pea float bumped the release button. The button sprang open the hatch on the bottom of the plane. Hundreds of roses spilled out of the plane and onto the runway.

"Good!" Barry told Vanessa. "Let it down, full forward."

"We're coming in too fast!" Vanessa said.

Barry's instincts told him exactly what to do. For the first time in his life he was *thinking bee*!

"Ready, boys?" Barry called to the bees. "Give me full reverse. Nose down. Bring your tail up. Rotate it around."

"This is insane, Barry!" Vanessa cried.

The plane was bobbing, spinning, and hovering!

"It's the only way I know how to fly!" Barry explained.

Bud Ditchwater watched in amazement from the control tower. Was he nuts—or was the plane flying like an insect?

"Get your nose in there!" Barry told Vanessa. "Aim for the center. Now drop it in!"

The plane hovered above the runway like a giant bee. Then it zigzagged its way down to the center of the flower, where it made a perfect landing!

Inflatable slides popped out the sides of the plane. Barry flew to the tarmac as Vanessa and the passengers slid down to safety.

"Barry, we did it!" Vanessa said. "You taught me how to fly!"

"We saved the flowers," Barry said in astonishment,

"and the people and the pollen!"

Vanessa offered her hand in a high five. But this time, Barry politely passed.

"Did you see the giant flower?" Adam asked as he hurried over to Barry.

"Of course I did!" Barry exclaimed. "That was genius, man!"

But Barry's job wasn't done yet. He fluttered onto the wing of the plane, where he addressed the swarm.

"Listen, everybody!" Barry called. "This runway is covered with the last pollen from the last flowers on earth. We're the only ones who make honey, pollinate flowers, and . . . dress like this."

A hum rose from the tarmac.

"So what do you say?" Barry shouted. "Follow me!"

He was about to take off when Buzz flew over.

"Hold on, Barry," Buzz said. "You earned this!"

Barry beamed as Buzz slipped a helmet and pollen jock jacket on him. Written across the back was the name *Barry Benson*.

"I'm a pollen jock!" Barry exclaimed.

The pollen jocks tossed Barry a stem-sucking gun. It was official. Barry Benson was ready for action. It was time to bring life back to Central Park.

"Oh, yeah!" Barry cried.

The bees descended upon the roses. They busily

collected pollen, then headed for the park.

"Mom, the bees are back!" a boy shouted.

As bees sprinkled pollen, brown patches of earth sprung into colorful gardens. Dried-out window boxes blossomed in every color of the rainbow. Even Vanessa's rooftop flowers bloomed back to life.

Before long, the bees of New Hive City were back in business. . . .

"We are now on the Benson flex time work schedule," Adam said to a tram full of young bees. He now led the tour of the Honex factory. "Which includes job rotation and a weekly day off!"

All the bees were busy—and happy.

But nobody was happier than Barry. He smiled as he flew alongside his pollen jock comrades, the warm sun on his face. He had finally found a place for himself, a purpose. And, in a human named Vanessa, he had found a true friend.

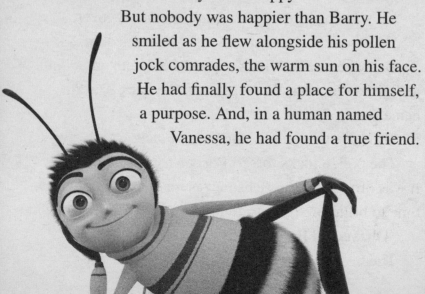